SPORTS STARS

BRETT HULL
THE INCREDIBLE HULL

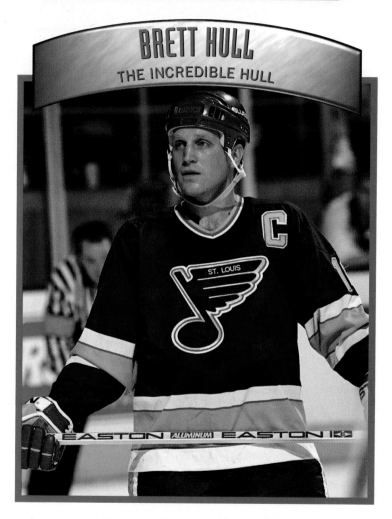

BY MARK STEWART

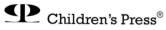 Children's Press®
A Division of Grolier Publishing
New York London Hong Kong Sydney
Danbury, Connecticut

Photo Credits

Photographs ©: Allsport USA: 43, 47 (Al Bello), 29, 40, 42, 45 top left (Glenn Cratty), 16 (Robert LaBerge), 12 (Rick Stewart), 14; AP/Wide World Photos: 10, 17, 35; Bruce Bennet Studios: 24, 37 (Bruce Bennet), 39 (M. Digirolamo), cover (A. Foxall), 45 top right (J. Giamundo), 6, 46 (M. Hicks), 19 (Scott Levy), 3 (S. Reyes), 27, 32, 33, 44 top right; C.W. Pack: 22; Danny Riedlhuber/The Calgary Sun: 25; Hockey Hall of Fame, Toronto, Ontario, Canada: 36; Rocky Widner: 28; Rudy Winston: 21 inset; University of Minnesota, Duluth: 21; UPI/Corbis-Bettmann: 11, 44 top left.

Library of Congress Cataloging-in-Publication Data

Stewart, Mark.
    Brett Hull: the incredible hull / by Mark Stewart.
      p. cm.–(Sports stars)
    Summary: A biography of hockey star Bobby Hull's son, Brett, who has been a leading scorer for the St. Louis Blues.
      ISBN 0-516-20484-X (lib. bdg.)   0-516-26049-9 (pbk.)
      1. Hull, Brett, 1964– –Juvenile literature. 2. Hockey players–United States–Biography–Juvenile literature. [1. Hull, Brett, 1964–. 2. Hockey players.] I. Title. II. Series.
GV848.5.H8S84   1998
796.962'092—dc21
[B]   96-39588
                                  CIP
                                  AC

© 1998 by Children's Press®, A Division of Grolier Publishing Co., Inc.
All rights reserved. Published simultaneously in Canada.
Printed in the United States of America.
1 2 3 4 5 6 7 8 9 10 R 07 06 05 04 03 02 01 00 99 98

⋆ CONTENTS ⋆

★ 1 ★

GOAL SCORER

At center ice in the Kiel Center, Brett Hull of the St. Louis Blues slaps the puck into the other team's end. The puck slides around the walled rink and stops behind the goal. Brett's teammate grabs it while Brett skates toward the blue line and looks for a pass. His teammate skillfully holds the puck as other defensemen try to jam it loose. Brett continues to circle, waiting for the right moment. Suddenly, Brett spots an open area of ice and sprints toward it. His teammate sees Brett's movement and slides the puck to meet him. In one motion, Brett takes the pass and fires a blistering shot on goal. Before the goalie can react, the puck streaks past him and slams into the back of the net. Goal!

Brett Hull is not a graceful skater or a master stickhandler. But he does score goals. Throughout his career, Brett has used a hard slap shot and terrific hockey instincts to become one of the highest goal scorers in the game.

GROWING UP

Being the son of a superstar can be both a blessing and a curse. Brett Hull learned this lesson at an early age. Brett's father, Bobby Hull, was considered the National Hockey League's top forward during the 1960s and was the best player on the Chicago Blackhawks. Brett and his brothers, Bobby Jr., Bart, and Blake, spent much of their young lives hanging around hockey rinks. At first, Brett was not sure that he wanted to wear skates. To him, they looked big, sharp, and scary. Besides, it was kind of fun to slide around on the ice wearing sneakers.

Brett's father, Bobby Hull, was a star on the Chicago Blackhawks.

One day, when Brett was about three, his father and a teammate held him down and forced him to put on his skates. He screamed and kicked and cried, but once Brett got used to skating, it was practically impossible to get him off the ice!

Bobby Hull could tell that young Brett had the talent to become a star. He was a strong and accurate shooter, and he was a willing pupil. "If I was doing something wrong," Brett recalls, "Dad would sit me down and say, 'Watch.' Then he would go out on the ice and show me how to do it right."

Brett and his family spent a lot of time together at hockey rinks. In this photograph, young Brett stands next to his father and watches the puck.

Although classmates made fun of his weight, Brett would later use his large size to push past opponents in the hockey rink.

★ ★ ★

Sadly, the one-on-one lessons ended when Brett was 13 and his parents separated. He, Blake, Bart, and his sister, Michelle, moved with their mother to Vancouver, Canada, while Bobby Jr. went to Alberta to play junior hockey. Brett rarely saw his father after the separation, and that made him sad. His interest in hockey faded, and he began to gain a lot of weight. In school, classmates made fun of him. Some called him "Huggy Bear" because he looked like a big stuffed animal. Others nicknamed him "The Pickle" for his shapeless body.

Brett kept his mind off his family's breakup by participating in sports. He played hockey in various local leagues, but he was not very serious. At the age of 17, when Brett should have been taking an important step in his hockey career, he was actually thinking about quitting the sport altogether. He was ready to play junior hockey, yet not a single junior team invited him to play. Brett's weight had slowed him down, and

Brett's greatest hockey skill is his ability to put the puck in the net.

he had a reputation for being lazy. "It's funny when I think of all the times coaches said I never worked to improve," says Brett, smiling. "Maybe I didn't work at the parts of the game they wanted me to play, but I surely worked at the game I wanted to play. I worked at being a scorer. And, as far as I know, you still win games by scoring more goals than the other team."

Brett decided to give hockey one last shot and tried out for the Penticton Knights of the British Columbia Junior Hockey League. Coach Rick Kozuback was impressed by Brett's play, and he put him on the team for the 1982–83 season.

This was a great opportunity, and Brett knew it. The Knights were a highly respected junior team. More important, Coach Kozuback demanded that his players work as hard on their studies as they did on their hockey. Brett's study habits had been very poor back home, but in his two years with the Knights, he began to see the importance of education. "My attitude about

Brett understands the importance of discipline and hard work.

school changed at Penticton," Brett says.
"Realizing I could earn a college scholarship, I
started to work harder on my grades. Doing well
in school was more important to the players in
Penticton than it had been with my friends back
home. I started doing my homework on the team
bus—accounting, English, math—and my grades
improved."

By the middle of Brett's first junior season, he was in good shape and playing the kind of hockey everyone had always expected. He became the team's top forward, scoring 48 goals. During his second year with the Knights, Brett truly hit his stride. He scored his 50th goal by Christmas and just kept going, finishing with 105 goals in 56 games to beat the old league mark by a whopping 22 goals.

During his second season with the Knights, Brett developed the goal-scoring skills he later used in the NHL.

During Brett's remarkable 1983–84 season, he began to exhibit some of his father's skills. Bobby Hull had possessed the hardest slap shot in the world. Now Brett was squeezing off shots at speeds approaching 100 miles per hour. In one game, he hit a puck so hard that his stick snapped in two. This is not unusual with wooden sticks, but Brett's stick was made of strong aluminum!

With his grades high and his hockey skills excellent, Brett was offered scholarships to several top universities. He also was drafted by the NHL Calgary Flames. For Brett, however, being courted by college recruiters was far more exciting. He turned down the Flames and accepted an offer from the University of Minnesota at Duluth (UMD).

Brett's slap shot is as hard and fast as his father's.

⋆ **3** ⋆

COLLEGE YEARS

Brett Hull chose UMD for all the right reasons. The UMD hockey team, the Bulldogs, had nearly won the 1984 NCAA title that spring. Many of its top players were returning for the 1984–85 season, which meant that Brett would have to earn his spot on the roster. But he was happy to fight for a place on such a talented team. There were two other reasons he chose UMD. First, he liked the small-town feel of Duluth, which is on the shores of Lake Superior. And second, Coach Mike Sertich understood that the player he was getting was Brett Hull, not "Bobby Hull's son."

In this atmosphere of competition and support, Brett developed rapidly into a great hockey player. He worked hard to improve his

Brett soon felt right at home at the University of Minnesota-Duluth.

Coach Mike Sertich

Brett became one of the greatest hockey players to play at Duluth.

★ ★ ★

mind and worked even harder to improve his body. When he was not going to class or studying, Brett followed a strict schedule of weight lifting, running, and dieting. He also worked seriously on his skating for the first time in his life.

The results were amazing. Brett set a school record for goals by a first-year player. He was also named Freshman of the Year by the Western Collegiate Hockey Association (WCHA). The Bulldogs won the WCHA championship that year and advanced to the NCAA playoffs.

When Brett's father called to say he wanted to attend one of the games, Brett was thrilled. Bobby Hull had not seen his son play hockey in years, and he believed that Brett resented him. Little did Bobby know, but Brett had tacked up an old bubble-gum card of his dad in his locker. Having made a name for himself, Brett was beginning to enjoy life as a hockey-playing Hull. In Brett's sophomore season at UMD, he set even more records. He became the first player in league history to tally 50 goals in a season, and he became the first Bulldog to average 2 points per contest, with a total of 84 in 42 games.

After Brett Hull's brilliant 1985–86 sophomore season at UMD, the Calgary Flames decided their sixth-round draft pick was ready to play in the NHL. They made Brett a tempting offer: a generous three-year contract plus a chance to join the team right away. The Flames were heading into the playoffs and had a good chance to win the Stanley Cup. Brett accepted Calgary's offer and gave up his remaining college eligibility. He says it was one of the toughest decisions of his life, and one of his biggest regrets.

Brett joins the Calgary Flames.

✴ 4 ✴

FEELING BLUE

When Brett suited up for the first time as a pro, he pulled on jersey number 16. Ironically, his father had worn the same number during his rookie year. To Brett's disappointment, the Flames' coaches chose not to play him right away. He sat on the bench until Game Three of the Stanley Cup Finals. Brett nearly made history when, on his very first shift, he fired a wrist shot toward Montreal Canadiens goalie Patrick Roy. The puck hummed past Roy and clanked against the post, robbing Brett of a goal. The Flames lost the game and Montreal went on to win the championship.

Brett spent most of his time with the Flames on the bench.

   Although they did not win the Stanley Cup,
the Flames celebrated their successful season
with a parade in Calgary. But Brett did not
participate. He had played only a few minutes,
and he did not feel he deserved to take credit
with the guys who had done all the work.

At the end of the 1987–88 season, Brett was traded to the St. Louis Blues.

Brett looked forward to helping the Flames win the championship in 1986–87. Instead, he spent a lot of time in the minor leagues. The next year, Brett made the Calgary team, but he mostly sat on the bench. Finally, Calgary decided to trade him to the St. Louis Blues in the final weeks of the 1987–88 season.

With the Blues, Brett started to play regularly for the first time in his professional career.

———— ★ ★ ★ ————

With a fresh start on a new team, Brett began to make his mark in the NHL. He worked hard on his skating and defense and earned a spot on one of the team's top lines. For the first time, Brett was able to get into the flow of the game, and he responded with a goal-scoring outburst that helped make him an All-Star. By season's end, he had collected 41 goals and 43 assists. Coach Brian Sutter was thrilled with his new superstar, but he believed Brett could be even better. He told Brett that he had the talent to score 40 goals every year, but that if he dug down deep, he might put up some truly awesome numbers. "It was a turning point for me," says Brett, who trimmed down to 195 pounds during the off-season and continued working on the finer points of his game. "My attitude up to that point was, 'Hey, I'm scoring, so they aren't going to get rid of me.'"

★ 5 ★

BREAK OUT

The 1989–90 season was a big one for the St. Louis Blues. Behind Brett's improved play, the team won more games than it lost for the first time in four years. Brett was unstoppable, racking up goals at a record pace. He scored 72 in all, establishing a new record for right wingers, and he was honored as a first-team NHL All-Star. Many hockey fans credited Brett's surge in production to his ability to score from anywhere on the ice, but Brett knew better. It was his improved skating and endurance that gave him an edge when others began to slow down. Another big factor was his linemate

In the 1989–90 season, Brett started scoring goals at a
record pace.

Brett and Peter Zezel made a great goal-scoring pair.

Peter Zezel, who had a knack for finding Brett
in the clear. When the Blues traded away
Zezel prior to the 1990–91 season, Brett had
nightmares about not being able to score. "I
wondered how I ever scored 72 goals the season
before," he says. "However, the fear began to
leave when I scored 7 goals in my first 7 games."

Brett continued his hot pace, scoring 22 goals in his first 21 games before busting loose with back-to-back hat tricks against the Toronto Maple Leafs. More importantly, the Blues were winning consistently. Soon, it became clear that Brett had a chance to do something that only four other NHL players had done: score 50 goals in 50 games. On January 25, 1991, he notched number 50 in the 49th game of the season to join all-time greats Maurice Richard, Mike Bossy, Wayne Gretzky, and Mario Lemieux as a member of the NHL's exclusive "50-50" club. Brett's father, Bobby, also scored 50 goals in 50 games with the Winnipeg Jets in the 1974–75 season, but the team played in the World Hockey Association (WHA) then, so his feat does not appear in the NHL record books.

Brett receives his teammates' congratulations after scoring his 50th goal in 49 games.

After the season, Brett was honored as the league's top performer, receiving the Hart Trophy from the hockey writers, and the Lester Pearson Award from his fellow players. At the award ceremony Brett's mother and father decided to put aside old differences and celebrate their son's achievements.

Brett's mother and father put aside their differences at Brett's award ceremony.

Brett and his father pose with the Hart Trophy and the Lester Pearson Award.

To be named the league's most valuable player was a special thrill, but to see his mother and father get along for the first time in nearly 20 years was a dream come true. Brett remembers, "Mom went up to dad and said, 'Congratulations. It's quite a feat to have a father and son who have both scored 50 goals and both won the Hart Trophy.' Dad thanked her. . . . 'Congratulations on having an award-winning son.'"

★ ★ ★

Brett learned an important lesson from his father. No matter how big a star you become, it is crucial to respect the fans. Brett personally autographs everything sent to him through the mail, and he sometimes spends an hour or more signing autographs after games. "Anyone in this business who doesn't take time for the kids should find another job," Brett says. "Fans are what the game is all about. My dad taught me that. No hockey player ever treated his fans with more respect than my father."

Brett continued his goal-scoring rampage in the 1991–92 season. He recovered quickly from a sprained ankle to find the net 70 times in 73 games. He led the league in goals a third straight time and was the top vote-getter in the All-Star balloting.

Brett signs autographs for his fans.

Brett's appearance in the offensive zone makes the opposing goalie nervous.

★ ★ ★

In the years since, Hull has barely slowed down. Teams now make a special effort to play him harder. They sense that the way to stop the Blues is to "shadow" their top scorer. But that is easier said than done. Brett's choppy strides and lumbering appearance mask an ability to be in the right place at the right time. When a defenseman turns away for an instant, Brett usually is gone by the time he turns back. And when Brett gets the puck near the net, he is deadly. In the four seasons following his three goal-scoring titles, he scored 183 times in 279 games. He has become the all-time leading goal scorer in St. Louis history.

★ ★ ★

A big source of Brett's popularity is his ability to have fun while playing hockey. Brett spends a lot of time on the ice smiling and joking with other players. "I don't approach the game as if I'm out there searching for a cure for cancer," Brett says. "I can't be that serious about it. I just try to have fun. And if you're having fun, you're probably playing at your best. I guarantee you it's fun being me . . . no one's having more fun than me. No one."

C ★ H ★ R ★ O ★ N

1964	• August 9: Brett is born in Belleville, Ontario.
1977	• Brett's parents separate, and Brett moves to Vancouver with his mother.
1982	• Brett plays for the Penticton Knights.
1984	• Brett is drafted by the Calgary Flames. He decides to attend the University of Minnesota at Duluth. In his freshman year, he scores 32 goals in 48 games.
1986	• Brett makes his NHL debut for the Calgary Flames during the Stanley Cup Finals.
1988	• In the final weeks of the 1987–88 season, Brett is traded to the St. Louis Blues.

O ⭐ L ⭐ O ⭐ G ⭐ Y

1988–89 • During his first year with the St. Louis Blues, Brett scores 43 goals.

1989–90 • Brett leads the league with 72 goals, makes the All-Star Team, and wins the Lady Byng Award for Most Gentlemanly Player.

1990–91 • Brett scores 50th goal of 1991–92 season in 49th game and wins the Hart Trophy as NHL MVP.

1991–92 • Brett again leads the league in goals scored with 70.

1996 • Brett leads the U.S. team to an upset of Canada in the hockey World Cup.